The Hospital Poems

(New and Selected)

By: Chad Smith

Every word in this book was written by me. No AI was used for ideas or editing.
This comes from the heart.

To find more books by me visit:

www.gattaca.world

Staten House

Copyright 2024

This one is for my kid. I know it's hard to be ill for long periods and spend so much time in the hospital, but I can only imagine how hard it must be to grow up seeing your parent sick. Two moments stand out in my memory. The first was when you were just five years old. During a long hospital stay, you walked in and asked, "Is my daddy going to die?"

The second is much more recent. I was in the ICU when it was time for you to leave for college. Without much hesitation, you went ahead and made the move to DC. Kid, your brilliant mind and relentless work ethic inspires me every single day. Words can't express how proud I am of you.

table of contents

Failing with Magic
The hospital corridor
And Again
Yellow ER Signs
Panic in the Wrong Place at the Wrong Time
Fireplace
ice cream and monkey bars
Waking 3am
rain
Cuts
Haunted By
A walk
collapsing
Is daddy going to die?
Some Nights
The Sky is Blue
That Black Night
The Surgeon
Invisible
a part a piece
Mulder and the X-Files
The cold white tile
The Pills
Bare
When I lost my Mind
ICU

helicopter nights
Scared of the Dark

On Letting Go
I fear
At   17
That Open Door

but here I am

*the metal
　　in the air*

here I am

"As a well spent day brings happy sleep, so life well used brings happy death."

- Leonardo da Vinci

"I carry the bars within me."

- Franz Kafka

Failing with Magic

*"They cannot fix you
they try and try..."*

- Hummel, Maria, author. "House and Fire.", by The American Poetry Review, 2003.

The arrogance
    of this man in white
        shining before me
in the grey light,
his confidence never seems to fade

even as I do.

The slow parade
of sleights of hand
they do nothing...

I cannot blink,
I see the other hand moving,
    the deceit,
as he fools himself
into thinking he can fix me.

He hands me new white pills,
        swallow these...

But they dry my mouth

    like the body of Christ on Sunday.

The hospital corridor

The machines beep.

at 3am
       lights are bright
              they look as if they have a green tint.

I unhook my machines
       and wander out of my room
       scanning and computer equipment line the hall.

No one else around
       I just wander.

Empty it feels
       but full of sleeping people.

I think of going outside
       I could pull it off
              maybe

I walk down to the ER
       and see a gunshot victim
       in emergency help
blood everywhere

"Just stop the bleeding"

I wish.

In another ER stall
        UV lights pulse off the walls
        disinfecting it
                from something
                        horrible.

The waiting room is crowded
        with people who need help.

Help.

I go back to my room
        and crawl into cold sheets.

Always the lights
they will be in soon for my blood
        more and more and more
                it never ends.

The machines beep.

And Again

"It was then I prayed, pleading with heaven."
- Hummel, Maria, author. "House and Fire.", by The American Poetry Review, 2003.

For the hundredth
thousandth
time
I've lost count
The sickness returns

No more
Not this time
Please

And the words come
Sliding off my lips
Mumbling
To a stone deaf god

I give up

Please, let me go
Just let this go

Please
        Please
                Please

Yellow ER Signs

I was in ER stall 8

across from me

this girl

in ER 4

    shakes violently

though she's asleep

A nurse comes in and says nice things to me

Later

    awake

I hear her screaming

    No one hears her

    but me

Later when she was gone

    I watched the deaf people
        clean the blood off the floor and walls

a nurse comes in

        I fall back to sleep

Panic in the Wrong Place at the Wrong Time

Raoul Duke:
"Panic. It crept up my spine like the first rising vibes of an acid frenzy."

- Thompson, H. S. (2005). *Fear and Loathing in Las Vegas*. HarperPerennial.

I can't breathe.

cold sweat pops up through my skin

    all over

my lower body vibrates

    my foot seizes and cramps

I shake

I can't breathe.

my heart races

I can't speak

try to slow it down

    try to slow it down

        try to slow it down

panting

    I start to cry

I can't breathe.

Fireplace

That day you fell and hit your head
On the grey and white stone fireplace
There was so much blood

You were so little
I held you like you were dying
Like darkness
All the way to the hospital

Stitches and cold x-ray rooms
And you were okay

That night
In the dark
                        I stared at the ceiling

ice cream and monkey bars

those bars

full of rust

and flaking off

      orange paint

that would sometimes dig into

      your palm   red

we flew

      we glided

            we felt the air

              cold

                        we felt freedom

one day

      I fell off

           I must have been 5 or 7

There was so much blood

Dr. Corey told me I was a tough kid

      for not crying while getting stiches.

Waking 3am

I would wake up
and watch the IV drip

drip

      drip

            drops into my blood

3:30am the kick

more morphine

I would think thoughts like

The rattlesnake woke up at midnight
to put my rooster in the oven

and fall back asleep

rain

        I always think of rain when I step over storm grates

        that time in New York when you fell into a subway vent

        wearing glitter red high heels

        we had to get you to the ER

        you shivered

        the doctor came in

with her long white gown

        wearing stiletto red shoes

Cuts

staring in the mirror

I look at

    the old cuts

        carved up skin

to remove organs

I once had dreams

    that I watched

        these operations

            awake

in the OR

the blood would

spit out of me

    onto the blue surgeon's gown

the cold metal bright light

    shining

        everywhere.

Haunted By

I wonder if the mattress
in this bed
is made of wood

and where will it go
when I am gone

or
who will lie here next?

and these tubes
pouring forth from my arms
the bubbles slowly descend
and I think of my blood
and you

the silence of your ghosts
are inside me
and I cannot shake them.

A walk

It is not fun
to stumble down a hospital hallway
hanging onto your IV pole.

It is on wheels and full of bags
bags of magic that don't do anything

But you go
step by step
towards the window at the end
blue sky and red leaves

just to turn back
for a dark room
and another pill
and another injection

then the dark.

collapsing

i remember going to see you
in the middle of the night
to watch you unwind
to buy some time
but the nightmare goes on
standing out here
the moon
hangs on to every last breath
of the dying night
casting its last glowing embers
on the sidewalk of an empty street.
downcast yellow lights from a passing car
echo on my eyelids closed in prayer
in this golden globe as I lose hope
that crashes to the tile floor
of your hospital room.

Is daddy going to die?

No. I am fine. Come talk to me

I can't lift my head off the bed

the little blonde child

rubs my arm full of IV tubes

but I say it's just medicine

making me better

        but I don't believe that

earlier today there was a code blue

a man ran screaming by

and was dragged back down the hall

        please fix her fix her he yelled

Some Nights

in this one trembling hospital

the shiny black air vents

      frighten me

If I climb out of bed

and put my ear to them

I can hear my neighbors

fighting

      about options

           about treatments

                about how to pay for this

                      of how to get through this

later

on the roof I hear a helicopter land

The Sky is Blue

and I wake up

      seeing

red orange yellow

      leaves

outside the window

I was dreaming of us

at a bed and breakfast in Maine

I had arrived early

      and was waiting for you

            on the porch

drinking red wine

down

      down

            down

more x-rays

and cold tables

outside in the hallway

      I hear a woman crying.

That Black Night

The surgery

        was over

            but my organs were failing

                they did not believe

I was swimming into

these beautiful blue waves

as my blood pressure dropped to

        40

              over

                    28

The lightning woke me

a nurse was pumping

fluid out of my bladder with a grey bulb

it hurt

        it hurt

I wanted to go swimming again.

The Surgeon

- For Joseph

He let me keep my iPod

    on the ride down

the hallway to the OR

I listened to

"Everything is Wrong"

by Moby

    preparing for an eight-hour surgery

The operating room was cold

and grey and green

the night before

I wrote

With a black sharpie

"Don't fuck this up"

on my stomach

he smiled

and then

always again

      the dark

a part a piece

a part
a piece
      the scraps fall onto the floor

I am the air inside an empty jar
I am the space inside an empty lock
I am the breath from a horse in Wyoming
      running before a storm

I am missing something
I ask what it is
      and no one knows.

a part
a piece
      the scraps fall onto the floor

my therapist looks at me
he switches my pills from red ones
      to blue ones

the pills fall onto the floor

      I fall onto the floor

           red and blue

a part
a piece
      the scraps fall onto the floor

Mulder and the X-Files

I've lost count of how many times
    Agent Mulder saved my life

his calming voice
    the echo of David Duchovny

turning the TV up
to drown out the beeps
    of the machines

in this cold hard hospital bed
    with no end in sight

no end
    from blood draws
no end
    according to the doctor's report
        this morning

but you calmed me
and helped me sleep

    more than the morphine ever did.

The cold white tile

On the hospital floor again
      I sink
           further in

and feel the cold
      I wonder if anyone has died in this spot

outside

a man is screaming for a blanket

my half-closed lids
gaze out across the floor

to the door closed

I
      shiver
           tremble
                quake
                      and smile

I close my eyes
      and fall into a dreamless sleep

but then dream

Of a shiny black night
      driving up a grey gravel driveway
I am the passenger
      the house is bathed in blue lights
           and dark iron gates hover

before

    me

and the floor again
      someone is speaking

The nurse who loves me
      rubs my shoulders
I crawl to my knees and she helps me
      back into bed.

She injects something into my IV

and I fall

    fall

        fall

cold air into the distance

The Pills

The pills that keep

my child alive

are blue and white

the ones that kept me alive

    at their age

were orange

I wonder

    if it scared

        if it hurt

my parents

    this much.

Bare

Staring up at the IV bags
I try to feel the drugs
mixing with my blood
does anything help?

Every day
you
put your fingers
around my wrist

and you smile
bright and hollow

But I know
what you are doing
feeling me get smaller,
wasting away,
checking the progress

Do my wrist bones
dig into your fingertips
more than yesterday?

Is it fast enough for you?

I turn over
and feel my hip bone
dig into the mattress.

Smiling, I close my eyes
and fall into the dark.

When I lost my Mind

I don't remember much
    the night I lost
        my mind

earlier that day
    cold in the
        rapids
            of the Ocoee River

the black rubber boat
    the thin rubber
        between us

the white roaring foam
    and drowning

suddenly
    a world of no

unable to speak
    move
        or dream

blue overhead
    frozen into forever

I cannot speak
I cannot breathe
I cannot move

frozen
    into the instant

remainders of blurs
    a yellow bus

                taking us back to camp

cold pin lemonade
        acrid on my tongue

blurs

waking up in your lap
        water everywhere
               but red

the ambulance is on the way
        you said

under fluorescent lights
        so much noise
               scramble

faces of masks
        move with manic speed

I start to let go.

ICU

every hour
      the blood pressure cuff
           tightens

every hour
      someone in blue
           walks in
                to take
                      more blood

eight bags
      some long
      some flat
           orange
                and
           clean
                and
           brown

they drip
      pouring into my veins,
           feeding me their silent stories.

the static hum
      of monitors
           constant

brilliant white

      this place never sleeps

helicopter nights

the roar
      incoming

off in the distance
      into now

I turn my head
      slowly

careful not to trigger
      the bed alarms

through the shades
      a night sky

a black and yellow blur
      lowering
            onto the pad

moments later
      it will ascend

attempting to save
      someone else.

Scared of the Dark

ICU madness
      they call it

there is no night
      or day

just the sad parade
      of doctors and nurses

pulling and prodding
      and stealing

constant
      the machines
           click
and pump and whine

out in the hallway
      shadows

On Letting Go

often easy to forget
    those times

        too often
        not blurs

too often
    red and blue and now
    flashes
        snapshots

squints into a recent past

the lights always on
    too bright

eyes and masks
    blocking the fluorescent

concern or fear

I cannot tell

fingers move
    across my body

a machine screams
    I start to cry

rapid now
    an injection
        into the tubes

    flowing into my body

a new bottle
      glass and white
           hung by my head

I feel my body
      squeezing and blank

and cold

a winter morning

blank.

I fear

the dream

that crushed up gravel

that road

of silver and white gravel

walking up that road

it feels more like grit

grinding

I fear I'm

letting go

this change

you were wounded less

and I

could not understand.

At   17

You looked so small

curled up in your hospital bed

      asleep

we were waiting for the video call

the psych call

      to get you out of the ER

           and into another facility

      you were so sleepy

      from your suicide attempt

You looked so small

I remembered you as this little blonde-haired boy

      so happy

           on a big pillow

You looked so small.

That Open Door

    at the end of the hallway

walls green

1989

a home for people
        who couldn't deal with

              others

I had to stay
        for 30 days

my roommates came and
        went

so many cutters
        so many scars

a variety of orange and white pills

in a world without
        shoes or shoelaces
            or TV

only puzzles of countryside views
        green and blue and red and white

no bathing
        without a nurse watching

standing in the shower room
        I would see

the water fall
        splash
on my ankles
           into the silver drain

one night
        the door ajar
             unlocked

I think I saw
        yellow petals on the floor

Epilogue

"Without health life is not life; it is only a state of languor and suffering—an image of death."

- Buddha

Acknowledgments

This collection would not have happened without the encouragement of my wife Amiee and my TIRELESS early readers and editors Anastasia Smith, Bryan Center and Andrew Virdin. I love all of you.

About the Author

Chad Smith is a consultant and author hiding out in the Caribbean.

Made in the USA
Columbia, SC
13 February 2025

53711684R00030